To ....

Welcome aboard the
Spooky Express!

From ....

THE SPOOKY EXPRESS

MARYLAND

A Halloween Thrill Ride

For Denise Shekleton.

Visit the author's website! http://ericjames.co.uk

Written by Eric James
Illustrated by Marcin Piwowarski
Designed by Sarah Allen

Copyright © Hometown World Ltd. 2017

Published by Sourcebooks Jabberwocky, an imprint of Sourcebooks, Inc.
P.O. Box 4410, Naperville, Illinois 60567-4410
(630) 961-3900
Fax: (630) 961-2168
jabberwockykids.com

Date of Production: May 2017
Run Number: HTW_PO130117
Printed and bound in China (GD)
10 9 8 7 6 5 4 3 2 1

THE SPOOKY EXPRESS
MARYLAND

Written by Eric James
Illustrated by Marcin Piwowarski

sourcebooks
jabberwocky

We were out trick-or-treating,
my best friend and I,
when we saw a huge shape
swooping down from the sky.

It circled around us
on train tracks of mist,
then it came to a stop,
and its large pistons hissed.

What a marvelous train,
engine black as the night!
All its carriages glowed
with a ghostly green light.

CHAOS IN CUMBERLAND

CINEMA

Tickets

LOLLI AND POPS

OPEN

And we both held our breath
when its loud whistle blew,
for the sound that it made
was a ghastly *Woo-wooooo!*

The door opened wide.
A conductor appeared
with a cheery old smile
that was not to be feared.

He said, "Spooky Express!
Hop aboard. Take a ride!"
"How exciting!" we thought,
and we climbed up inside.

There were mummies in tatters,
and witches in hats,
and ogres, and werewolves,
and vampire bats!

There were **big** trolls
from Gaithersburg
towering in size,
and aliens from Lanham
with bright, bulging **eyes.**

ANNAPOLIS

SILVER SPRING

OAKLAND

BETHESDA

A voice on the speaker said,
"Please hold on tight!"
Then the train gave a lurch
and launched into the night.

We glided along
through a stormy night sky,
and we watched as the dark streets
of Frederick *whizzed* by.

We zipped over Baltimore,
saw its bright lights,
and glimpsed College Park
from a dizzying height.

The ride was fantastic,
but *where* were we going?
We sped ever onward
with no signs of slowing.

"Back River, next stop,"
said the train's engineer.
"Make room for the creatures
who'll swim aboard here."

SPLASH!

He slammed on the brakes
and I thought we would crash,
but we dropped like a stone
and the whole train went SPLASH!

BACK
RIVER

Then after the river,
another strange stop:
up a really tall tower,
on the side...near the top!

Then in Crystal Grottoes,
where big ogres dwell,

then down in old sewers
(oh, the sewer-folk smell!).

As we raced to our next stop
the train turned too fast,
and I saw, through the window,
a **pumpkin** *whizz* past!

The ghosts started howling.

"What happened?" I said.

"We're doomed!" cried a witch.

"That's the engineer's head!"

If the engineer's headless
he can't steer the train,
for his head's where he keeps
both his eyes and his brain!

He yanked levers forward.
He jerked levers back.
The train started wobbling
all over the track!

We swerved around buildings.
We darted past trees.
The speed of the turns
made us weak at the knees.

While everyone panicked,

I stood up and said,

"With the help of some friends,

we can go get that head!"

"Miss Witch," I said calmly,

"your broom, if I may?

Miss Spider, Miss Dragon,

let's go save the day!"

The engineer's head
was in Gambrill State Park.
"Miss Dragon," I said,
"will you light up the dark?"

"It's there!" said my friend.
"It's directly below.
But it's down in the mud,
and it's stuck there.
Oh, no!"

GAMBRILL
STATE PARK

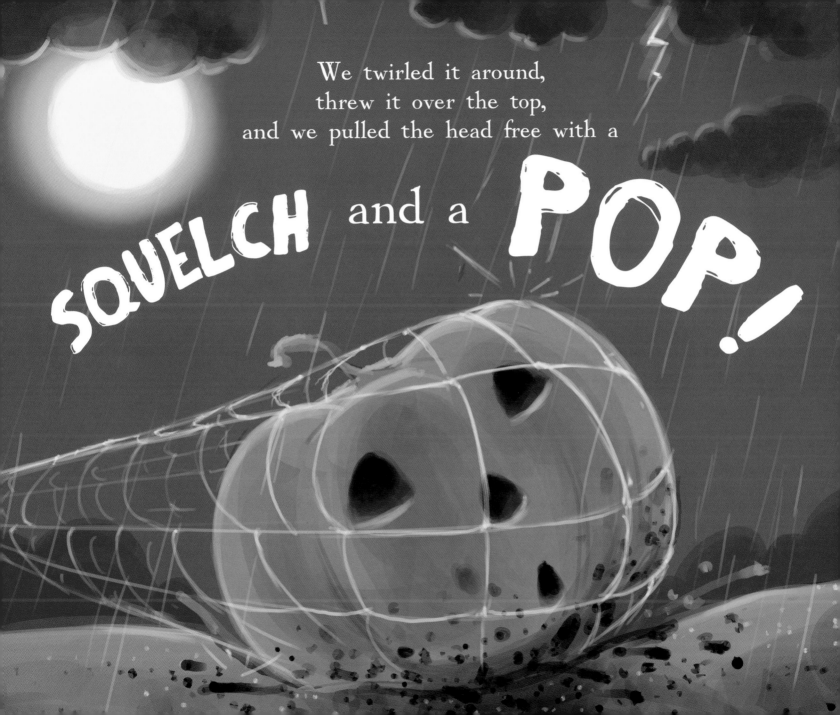

We twirled it around,
threw it over the top,
and we pulled the head free with a

SQUELCH and a POP!

Then back we all flew,
through the wind and the rain,
with the pumpkin containing
the engineer's brain.

With his head in our hands, we jumped back on the train, and we stuck his head onto his shoulders again!

He pulled a few levers. The ghost train slowed down. Do you know where we were?! We were back in

OUR TOWN!

The ghosts started howling,
(this time with delight!),
and the gnomes hugged an alien
(a little *too* tight!).

The wizards shot sparks
that were orange and green,
and they cried, "Well done, children!
You've saved Halloween!"

"We'd be *stuck* on this train,
had you not been so daring!
But now we can stop in each town
and go **scaring!**"

We jumped off the train,
none the worse for our fright.
This had certainly been
the **best** Halloween night.

The train started moving.
Its large pistons hissed.
It circled around us
on train tracks of mist.

It launched itself skyward.
Its loud whistle blew,

Happy Halloween